The Trouble
with Liberty

The Trouble
with Liberty

Kristin Butcher

Orca Soundings

ORCA BOOK PUBLISHERS

Library and Archives Canada Cataloguing in Publication

Butcher, Kristin
The trouble with liberty / Kristin Butcher.
(Orca soundings)

ISBN 10: 1-55143-274-9 / ISBN 13: 978-1-55143-274-8

I. Title. II. Series.
PS8553.U6972T76 2003   JC813'.54   C2002-911419-5
PZ7.B9691TR 2003

First published in the United States, 2003
Library of Congress Control Number: 2002115797

Summary: Liberty is the new girl at school, and everyone wants to be her friend.
When she accuses a teacher of assault, doubts start to surface about her motives.

*Orca Book Publishers is dedicated to preserving the environment and has printed
this book on paper certified by the Forest Stewardship Council®.*

Orca Book Publishers gratefully acknowledges the support for its publishing
programs provided by the following agencies: the Government of Canada
through the Canada Book Fund and the Canada Council for the Arts,
and the Province of British Columbia through the BC Arts Council
and the Book Publishing Tax Credit.

Cover photography by dreamstime.com

ORCA BOOK PUBLISHERS
PO Box 5626, Stn. B
Victoria, BC Canada
V8R 6S4

ORCA BOOK PUBLISHERS
PO Box 468
Custer, WA USA
98240-0468

www.orcabook.com
Printed and bound in Canada.

14 13 12 11 • 7 6 5 4

For Sheri—my sister and friend.

Chapter One

Forget the grizzly bear.

It should be blue jeans on the *Welcome to Sutter's Crossing* sign. Instead of *Grizzly Country*, it should say *Blue Jean Capital of Canada.* I've lived in Sutter's Crossing my entire life, and the only place I've ever seen a grizzly bear is on that sign. Blue jeans, on the other hand, I see all over the place.

I slid some coins across the counter of the concession and took a long drink of icy Coke.

Ow, ow, ow! Instant brain freeze.

I closed my eyes until the pounding stopped. Then I took a good look around the rodeo grounds. There were blue jeans everywhere. Even old Granny Wicks was wearing jeans—not pants, but a blue jean skirt, and for an eighty-year-old lady that's just as good.

I wished my mom was there to see that. It might have helped my case. My mother and I had been fighting about jeans for the last three weeks. She hates them. In her whole life I don't think she's ever owned a pair. I, on the other hand, happen to like jeans. And when we go into Kamloops to buy back-to-school clothes, that's what I want to get. But Mom's holding out for skirts and dress pants.

I can't believe she's serious. I'd be laughed right out of the school! She should know that. She works in the school office, and unless she's been typing and filing with a blindfold on, she has to know that normal fifteen-year-old girls don't wear skirts and dress pants. They wear jeans!

From somewhere above me a loud-speaker voice jumped into the air with the hotdog smell. "Ladies and gentlemen, once again it's time to return to the grandstand. The calf-roping will be starting in five minutes. So find your seats and get ready to enjoy some championship competition."

I glanced at my watch. I still had half an hour before my babysitting shift at the Kiddy Korral. If Cody was one of the first contestants, I could cheer him on.

The grandstand was already filled by the time I got there, and the people were still coming, so I quickly grabbed a spot along the fence.

The first competitor was Wayne Caruthers, a regular on the rodeo circuit.

He and his horse, Phantom, were in position behind the barrier. I looked toward the chute, trying to anticipate the exact second the calf would be released into the corral. Not that it mattered. The cowboy couldn't leave the barrier until the calf crossed the score line.

As the chute opened, the horse's ears perked up and he pawed the dirt, but he made no move to leave the barrier. He knew what to do every bit as well as Caruthers did. The bawling calf trotted forward amid whoops and whistles from the crowd. Cowhands along the side yipped and waved their hats in an effort to get it moving in the right direction. As soon as it crossed the score line, horse and rider sprang into action.

As Phantom galloped into the open, Caruthers readied his lasso. In ever-widening circles it arced above his head. Then, like a rattlesnake striking, it shot forward and looped around the calf's neck. Phantom dug in his hooves and the rope became taut. At the same instant, Caruthers jumped to the ground and began running down the rope. The calf bawled some more. But before it could make a move to free itself, Caruthers threw it to the dirt and tied its legs together with his pigging string. The crowd roared its approval.

The time clock showed 11.8 seconds. It was a good time and held up easily through the second and third competitors.

I glanced at my watch and leaned over the fence to see who was next. If it wasn't Cody, he was going to have to win without the benefit of my cheering. But I couldn't see past the people lining the fence, so I climbed onto a rail and cupped my hands around my eyes to block out the sun.

And proceeded to fall into the corral—well, almost. If the man standing next to me hadn't grabbed my arm, I would have done a header for sure.

Embarrassed, I thanked him and went to step down. But there was nowhere to step down to! My little patch of ground had disappeared. It hadn't actually gone anywhere, but there was someone else standing on it. From the way that someone wasn't making the slightest attempt to give me any room, I wondered if I'd had help losing my balance.

My glare was wasted on the top of the girl's head. But her appearance wasn't wasted on me. She looked like she'd walked straight out of a fashion magazine—long blond hair, tanned skin and white designer jeans.

"Excuse me," I said, dropping down to earth so deliberately that the girl had no choice but to squeeze closer to the person on her other side. It didn't help. I landed on her foot anyway. I glanced down at the dirty imprint of my runner on what seconds before had been a snowy white canvas shoe.

The girl spun around.

"Oh. Sorry," I cooed. I wished I'd worn my cowboy boots.

For a split second the girl's eyes flashed and I steeled myself for a fight, but just as quickly her expression softened and she smiled. She didn't even look down at her shoe.

"It's my fault," she said. "I didn't realize anyone was standing here." Then she turned her smile on the person beside her, and everyone skooched down to make more room.

Since I'm five foot five, it's hard to believe she hadn't seen me standing on the fence. And unless she thought I was nailed up there, she had to have known the ground below was mine. But I wasn't looking for an argument, and the loud-speaker guy had announced Cody, so I just shrugged and looked back into the corral.

That doesn't mean I forgot she was there. I was too curious for that. For one thing, the girl looked to be about my age, yet I'd never seen her before. For another thing, the whole time I was cheering Cody on, I could feel her watching me.

"Way to go, Cody!" I yelled when he'd finished. He hadn't beaten Caruthers' time, but he was sitting second. He looked over and waved.

"Your boyfriend?" the girl said, trying to sound casual.

She wasn't fooling me for a second, and I almost laughed in her face. But then I'm used to girls drooling over my brother. Broad shoulders and a cowboy hat have a way of turning some girls' brains to mush.

I shook my head. "He's my brother."

Those were the magic words. The girl's body relaxed and I could almost see her claws retracting. "Oh," she smiled. "He was really good."

I relaxed a little too. I stuck out my hand and said, "I'm Val MacQueen."

"Liberty Hayes."

"So what brings you to Sutter's Crossing?" I asked. "On vacation?"

She shook her head. "Actually, I just moved here."

My interest perked up. "Really? What grade are you going into?"

"Ten."

"Me too. If you like, I can introduce you to the other kids."

She glanced meaningfully across the corral to where Cody was standing.

I may not be the class brain, but I'm not an idiot either. I got the hint. I rolled my eyes and sighed, "*And* my brother."

Chapter Two

Liberty and I spent the last week of summer hanging out together. She didn't know anyone else in town, and I was happy to have someone besides Cody to talk to. Sutter's Crossing isn't what you'd call a bustling metropolis. According to the welcome sign, the total population— not including the baby Mrs. Hooper is expecting next month—is 2,633.

And hardly any of those people live in town. So school is pretty much the only place I see my friends, and since it was summer vacation, I hadn't had a whole lot of contact with anyone for ages. Except for Cody, and he doesn't count.

Well, not to me anyway. He seemed to make quite an impression on Liberty though. But as I said before, most girls like Cody. Cody seemed to be interested in Liberty too. He didn't ask her out or anything, but he was pretty generous with his smile. And he didn't seem to mind us hanging around even though we're two years younger.

It wasn't just Cody who warmed up to Liberty. My whole family thought she was great. If Liberty had shown up at the front door when I wasn't there, they would have hauled her in anyway. She even came with Mom and me when we went clothes shopping—*and* she convinced my mom to let me get jeans.

Liberty used exactly the same arguments I'd used, but for some reason they sounded different coming out of her mouth, and Mom bought them. In a way, that bugged me, but since I got the jeans, I didn't complain.

My mother is the secretary at Clarence Cobb Regional Secondary, so Cody and I usually ride to school with her. On that first morning we picked Liberty up too.

I took one last look in the mirror before leaving the house. My jeans fit perfectly and my new white blouse really showed off my tan. My hair even looked okay for a change. It was still a mousy brown, but that morning I'd taken the time to blow it dry, and there seemed to be twice as much of it. I turned my head and watched it swish across my shoulders. Then I stuck my face so close to the mirror that my breath made little fog clouds on it. I studied every inch of my skin. Not a single zit.

I stepped back and smiled at my reflection.

"Not bad," I told myself. "Not bad at all."

But once we picked Liberty up, my confidence started to evaporate. How could someone make jeans and a T-shirt look *that* good?

Liberty slid into the backseat beside me. "You look fantastic, Val!" she smiled. "I love your hair." But before I could return the compliment, she went on, "I'm so nervous."

About what? I wanted to say. *Being too rich?* Liberty's family had moved into the old Bartlett mansion on Kokanee Lake Road, and the place was worth a mint, so her parents obviously had money. Maybe she was worried about being too pretty. How about too tanned? Having too many designer clothes? *NOT!* As far as I could tell, Liberty had *everything* going for her. I wouldn't have thought she'd been nervous a single minute in her entire life. But I have to admit there was a teeny-tiny little green part of me that was happy to hear that she was.

Cody was driving. I glanced up to see him staring at Liberty in the rear-view mirror. Talk about a lovesick cow!

"*Moooooooo!*" I let out a long mournful bellow.

Cody didn't even hear me. He just kept staring.

"Hey!" I tried again. "You behind the wheel! You think maybe you might want to watch the road for a while?"

This time I got through, and Cody's cheeks turned into two squashed tomatoes.

"For your information, Miss Know-It-All," he retorted, looking away, "a driver has to be aware of what's happening behind the vehicle as well as in front of it."

"Oh, please!" I sneered. "You want me to believe you were looking out the back window? *As if!*"

"Valerie Gail MacQueen, that's enough," Mom cut short the argument. "Nobody likes a backseat driver."

I could see Cody laughing at me in the rearview mirror. I was dying to give him a piece of my mind, but Mom had used every one of my names, so I knew she wasn't kidding around. I sent Cody a *this-isn't-over-so-don't-think-you've-won* glare and slouched back on the seat.

"I really appreciate the ride, Mrs. MacQueen," Liberty said to fill the suddenly dead air in the car. "The thought of getting on a bus full of kids I've never met is kind of scary."

Mom smiled. "You're very welcome, Liberty. It's perfectly natural to be a bit anxious your first day. But trust me—you're going to be fine. By four o'clock you'll have made so many friends you'll wonder why you ever worried about it."

Mom sure knew what she was talking about—except that it didn't take until four o'clock. By the time the school bus dropped off the last kids, Liberty was in the middle of the action. If there'd been a vote for the most popular girl, she would have won hands down.

In a weird way, I was proud about that. Not that I was responsible for the other kids liking her, but since I was the one who'd introduced her to everybody, I felt like she was my own personal discovery. I know that's dumb, but it's how I felt.

As I watched the group around her growing, I kept one eye on the bus. I wanted to see Ryan as soon as he got off. Since our first day of grade one, when he stuck his tongue out at me and I clobbered him with my Barbie lunch kit, we have been the best of buds. Last year I even started thinking I liked him as a boyfriend, but the feeling passed in a couple of weeks. Luckily I hadn't let Ryan know.

"Ryan!" I yelled, jumping up and down so he'd see me through the crowd. "Over here."

He waved back and gradually talked his way toward me.

"Hey, stranger," I grinned, giving him a hug.

"No stranger than you," he grinned back. "So how was your summer? Did you get married?"

I shook my head and made a face.

"Join a rock band?"

"No time. I was too busy being my mother's slave. What about you? How was California?"

He shrugged. "Fine. But being chased by beach bunnies and hot young starlets gets boring after a while."

"Yeah, right!" I groaned. "Seriously, what did you—?"

"Ryan!" Matt Bryson, Jeremy Swailes, Sean Abernathy and a bunch of other guys pushed through the kids surrounding Liberty. "Hey, man, long time no see. How ya doin'?" They swarmed past me like I was invisible, and before I knew it, I was staring at a wall of backs.

I looked around, assessing the situation. On my left, a circle of kids was gathered around Ryan, and on my right there was another circle buzzing around Liberty.

And I was all by myself.

"How rude," I muttered. The situation definitely called for a change. I pushed my way through the guys and grabbed Ryan's hand.

"Come on," I said, "I want you to meet someone."

Chapter Three

I phoned Ryan as soon as I got home from school. After I'd introduced him to Liberty, he'd suddenly disappeared. I hadn't had another chance to talk to him all day.

"What do you think?" I pounced as soon as he picked up the phone. I could hear him suck in his breath.

"Well…" He stretched the word out as far as it would go. "I think math is going to be really tough this year. I also think the seats on the bus need some padding. I think I like raspberry yogurt better than peach, and I—"

"Ryan!" I cut him off. "That's not what I mean, and you know it. What do you think of Liberty?"

He purposely misinterpreted that question too. "I think every person has the right to liberty and the pursuit of happiness."

"Ryan!" I was getting exasperated. "Stop kidding around. What do you think of Liberty Hayes?"

"I don't."

"What do you mean—you don't?"

"I don't think about her."

I growled through my teeth. "Why are you being so difficult?"

"I'm not," he growled back. "You asked me a question, and I answered it—honestly. I don't think about her. Why should I? She's already got half the guys in the school drooling over her. She doesn't need me too."

I was totally stunned. This wasn't the reaction I'd expected at all. Ryan was acting like a horse with a burr under its saddle. The question was *why*?

"I thought you'd like Liberty," I said.

"Why?"

"Why not?" I shot back.

He let out a long sigh. "I'm just not into those kinds of games."

Now he'd lost me completely. "What games? Ryan, what are you talking about?"

He sighed again. "Nothing. Just forget it."

And that was the end of that. No matter how many times I asked, he refused to say another word on the subject.

Wonderful! Ryan and Liberty were both my friends. All I wanted was for them to be friends with each other. But from the way Ryan was acting,

you'd think I was asking him to dive into
a swimming pool of piranhas. Hopefully
Liberty was more open-minded.

"So, how do you like school so far?"
I asked her as the two of us wandered
the aisles of McCormack's Drugstore
the following Saturday.

She picked up a bottle of cologne,
sprayed it into the air and then wrinkled
her nose at the smell.

"It's okay," she said, trying to wave
away the sickly sweet cloud hanging
above her head. "I'd like it better if there
were no classes."

"Who wouldn't?"

"But otherwise it's good," she said.
"The kids seem nice."

That was the opening I'd been
waiting for.

"Yeah," I agreed. "They are. Take
Ryan Wilson, for instance. No matter

how grumpy I am, he can always make me laugh. He's so funny."

Liberty was poking through the lipstick testers. "Yeah—hilarious," she mumbled. It was clear she didn't think he was funny at all.

My back stiffened. "Obviously you don't like him," I snapped.

Liberty looked startled. "I never said that."

"You didn't have to," I scowled. I turned away and pulled the cap off a tube of Orange Sherbet lipstick.

I could feel Liberty staring at me.

"What's the big deal?" she said. "Are you trying to match me up with him or something?"

"Of course not!" I retorted.

"Well, then why do you care if I like him?"

I shrugged, suddenly feeling stupid.

To my surprise, Liberty laughed. "Don't have a cow then. I don't have anything against Ryan. I don't want him for a boyfriend, but otherwise he's fine."

It wasn't exactly the response I was hoping for, but it was more encouraging than Ryan's had been. I sighed and went back to picking through the lipsticks.

"Here's one," I said, turning the tube upside down. "Frosty Flirty Flip. How's that for a name?" I held it up to Liberty. "I bet this would look really good on you."

Liberty rubbed some onto the inside of her wrist and looked at it.

"It's not bad," she said. "I could wear it with the new blouse my dad brought me from New York."

"Good idea." I grinned. "Wear it to school on Monday and see if you can catch Cody's attention."

An impish gleam lit up Liberty's eyes. "Oh, it would catch his attention all right. His and the principal's too."

I giggled. "Ooh, that kind of a blouse, eh? A little too sexy for math?"

Liberty grinned. "Math and every other class." She paused and a dreamy look came over her face. "Except maybe for band."

"Hello?" Liberty was obviously hinting at something, but I had no idea what.

"Oh, come on, Val. Don't play dumb."

I frowned and shook my head. "Who's playing? I have no idea what you're talking about."

She rolled her eyes and clucked her tongue. "The band teacher? Mr. Henderson? The guy is a total hunk! Don't tell me you haven't noticed."

"Are you serious?" I sputtered. "He might be good-looking, but he's also like thirty years old. *And* he's married. He's got a kid."

Liberty shrugged. She pouted at the mirror on the sunglass stand and rolled some Frosty Flirty Flip onto her lips.

"You're right," she said, admiring the effect. "This lipstick does look good on me. And you know what?"

I shook my head.

"I bet Mr. Henderson would look good on me too."

My mouth dropped open, but the only thing that came out of it was a squeak.

That did it for Liberty. She keeled over laughing. "Kidding!" she said, between guffaws. "I was teasing. Val MacQueen, you are so gullible."

Somehow I managed to close my mouth again and trailed after Liberty to the hair color aisle.

"You're not going to dye your hair, are you?" I asked in horror. Liberty was a natural blond, and there seemed something immoral about messing with that.

"No," she murmured absently as she picked up one of the boxes and began reading the back. Then she added, "We're going to color yours."

Once again my mouth dropped open. Then I took a step backward and put up my hands. "Oh, no we're not. My mother will kill me if I come home with blue or green hair."

"Don't be silly." She rolled her eyes. "We're not going to *change* your color. We're just going to liven it up a little."

"Liven it how?" I asked suspiciously, still keeping my distance.

"With highlights," she beamed. "You want to look gorgeous for my party, don't you?"

This was news to me. "What party?"

Liberty smiled smugly. "The one I'm going to throw next weekend so I can wear my new blouse and get to know Cody better. I like the strong silent type, but your brother is a little too silent. I think he could use a push. And a party is just the thing. We can invite Joel and

Marissa, Shelly, Matt Bryson, Melanie Shepherd, Sarah Shaw, Jeremy, Sean Abernathy, and that guy in our English class with the pierced eyebrow. What's his name?"

"Kevin Halloran."

"Right," she nodded. "Also Wanda Watts, Chelsea and her boyfriend, and Sue and…you and Cody, of course." She pursed her mouth in concentration. "Who else?"

"Ryan?" I said.

Liberty slapped her forehead. "Right. Ryan. How could I forget him?"

Chapter Four

Cody convinced Dad to let him use the truck Friday night. It's not exactly a limousine, but there are seatbelts for three people, so I figured we could give Ryan a ride too. Since I'd been hanging out with Liberty, I'd barely seen him. This would give us a chance to catch up.

"Okay," Cody conceded grudgingly. For some reason he seemed to think potential passengers required his approval. "Tell him we'll pick him up at eight. But he better be ready. I don't want to wait around."

As it turned out, that wasn't a problem. Ryan didn't need a ride. He wasn't going to Liberty's party.

"What do you mean—you're not going? Everybody's going."

"Then you won't miss me," he said, stuffing some books into his locker.

Suddenly I had an uncomfortable thought. "You *were* invited, weren't you?"

He nodded. "More or less."

"What does that mean?"

Ryan grabbed his jacket and slammed the locker shut. "Look, Val," he said impatiently, "Liberty may have invited me, but she doesn't really want me there. And I wouldn't have a good time. I'm not going."

"How can you say that? All your friends will be there."

He shook his head. "Don't you mean all *Liberty's* friends?"

I opened my mouth to protest, but he cut me off.

"I'd love to stay and argue with you some more, but I'm going to miss my bus. See ya Monday."

And before I could even say good-bye, he bolted down the hall.

Cody and I were the first ones at the party. Liberty told us to come early so we could help with the last-minute preparations, but I think she just wanted Cody to see her New York blouse before everyone else did.

Actually, *not* see it was more like it. The blouse had long sleeves and buttoned all the way to the neck. But—except for some strategically placed embroidered flowers—it was totally sheer. And Liberty wasn't wearing a bra!

I'm not saying she didn't look great. She did. Judging from the way Cody's eyes bugged out, he thought so too. It's just that the blouse was a little too New York for Sutter's Crossing. I know I wouldn't have had the nerve to wear it. And even if I had, my parents would never have let me out of my room.

Which is why I was having trouble understanding how Liberty's father could have bought it for her, and how her mother could let her wear it. Of course that was assuming her mom and dad thought the same way mine did. But the truth is that until that night I hadn't met either of Liberty's parents, so I had no idea how their minds worked.

Liberty's dad was out of town, so it was just Mrs. Hayes chaperoning. If you call supervising from another part of the house chaperoning. Not that she wanted to spend the evening in her bedroom. That was Liberty's idea. She told her mother point-blank to stay away from the party. I heard her with my own ears.

If I'd said that to my parents, I'd have been the one spending the evening in my room. But Mrs. Hayes didn't argue. She just poured herself a drink and left.

I watched her climb the stairs. She was so different from Liberty that it was hard to believe they were related. When Liberty walked into a room, she instantly took it over. She didn't even have to say anything. People were just naturally drawn to her. Not Mrs. Hayes though. You could have dressed her in flashing neon and she still would have blended in with the wallpaper. Compared to Liberty, she was practically invisible.

Everyone started arriving as soon as Mrs. Hayes went upstairs, and in no time the rec room was jumping. Kevin Halloran planted himself in front of the pinball machine the second he walked into the house and didn't leave it all night. A couple of other guys latched onto the pool table, and the rest of us spent the night filling our faces and dancing. There was no way we could talk over the music. I kept waiting for Liberty's mom to show up and tell us to turn it down, but she never did.

It was a pretty good party. Everybody seemed to be enjoying themselves—especially Liberty and Cody. I don't think the two of them spent two minutes apart the whole night. During the slow songs, they were glued at the lip.

So it was no big surprise when Liberty dragged me off to the kitchen near the end of the evening to announce that she and Cody were officially *exclusive*.

"Isn't it great!" she bubbled.

"Fantastic!" I agreed. Liberty was so excited she couldn't stop bouncing. It was hard to believe my brother could have that effect on someone. "Looks like you were right about giving Cody a little push," I said. Then I noticed a couple of the guys staring at Liberty and grinning. I stepped into their line of vision and whispered into Liberty's ear. "I think maybe you better stop hopping around. You're jumping right out of your blouse—if you know what I mean."

"Oops!" she giggled. She rearranged herself so that all her flowers were where they were supposed to be. "I'm just so happy! And I wanted you to be the first to know. After all, you are my best friend." Then she threw her arms around my neck.

That's when Cody showed up. "Hey," he teased, "hugs are supposed to be reserved for me."

Liberty let go of me and wrapped herself around him instead. She gazed up into his face.

"Don't worry, Cody. You can have all the hugs you want," she assured him.

As I watched them melt into one another and then back onto the dance floor, I thought about what Liberty had just said. She'd called me her best friend. I hadn't expected that. Liberty was the most popular girl in school, so I was flattered. But it also made me feel a little bit like a traitor. I already had a best friend.

"Ryan is becoming a real jerk."

Who said that? I glanced around, but I was the only one in the kitchen. Then I heard the voice again. It was coming from the hall.

I listened more closely. It was Wanda Watts.

"Liberty asked me to tell him about the party, and when I did, he said he wasn't interested. It's like he's suddenly too good to hang around with the rest of us."

Then I heard another voice. It was Melanie Shepherd. "Maybe he figured Liberty should have invited him herself."

"Oh, please!" Wanda groaned. "The way he's been giving everyone the cold shoulder, he's lucky he got invited at all. I don't know what his problem is, but he's really getting to be a drag."

Melanie sighed. "I guess you're right. Even Val isn't hanging out with him anymore, and they've been friends forever."

I cringed. Some friend.

Chapter Five

I must have started to phone Ryan ten times that weekend. I just never went through with the call.

What would I say? *Sorry I've been such a crummy friend? I've been having so much fun with Liberty that I didn't miss you?* Even though it was true, I somehow doubted that admitting it would help either of us feel better.

Besides, it made it seem like the situation was my fault. And it *wasn't!* I'd been the one trying to get everyone together. It was Ryan who'd pulled away from the group. So really, this whole mess was *his* fault. But I didn't want to say that either. After all, he was my friend, and friends aren't supposed to hurt each other—at least not on purpose.

So I crossed my fingers and decided to wait until Monday. Hopefully the problem would solve itself. Ryan isn't normally an ornery person, and with the weekend to think things over, he might have mellowed out.

When I saw him get off the bus, though, he seemed anything *but* mellow.

"What happened to you?" I said. "You look like you were hauled through a knothole backward."

"Nothing that much fun," he mumbled, dragging his hands down his cheeks and giving his head a shake. "I was up all night with Hercules."

"Why? What's wrong with him?" Ryan had raised Hercules from a colt, and I knew how much he meant to him.

"A bad case of colic," he said, yawning. "I walked him all night. We must have put in thirty miles around the corral."

"What does the vet say?"

He shook his head. "Doc Jensen's away. But his wife says he should be back this morning, and she'll send him over the second he gets in. Dad's keeping an eye on Herc until then."

Ryan closed his eyes and leaned his head on the locker.

"So how come you came to school?" I demanded. "You should be home in bed."

"History test third period, remember?" he said without opening his eyes. "After that I'm outta here."

During homeroom I did my best to keep Ryan awake. Despite my efforts he kept nodding off. Then I headed to English and he stumbled off to math. I shook my head as I watched him stagger down the hall. I didn't see how he was ever going to survive until history.

Band was second period. I was one of the last to arrive, but when I looked around for Ryan, I couldn't see him anywhere. I took my place in the wood-wind section beside Liberty.

"Have you seen Ryan?" I whispered.

She frowned and shook her head. "Shhhhh." Then she directed her attention back to whatever it was Mr. Henderson was saying.

I put my clarinet together and pulled out my music. I kept one eye on the door, waiting for Ryan to stumble through it. But he never did. By the end of the period I'd begun to think maybe he'd gone home after all. Either that or he'd sneaked off to do some last-minute cramming. Well, history was next, so I'd soon find out.

I gathered up my books and clarinet and waited for Liberty. But for some reason she seemed to be suffering from slow-motion disease.

"Will you hurry up?" I grumbled. "We have a test—remember? And knowing Mrs. Adams, it'll be a killer. I'm going to need all the time I can get." I waved at her instrument. "You haven't even taken apart your clarinet yet!"

"I know," she said, picking it up. "I need to ask Mr. Henderson about it."

"Ask him what?"

"About one of the valves. It keeps sticking, and the note comes out wrong."

I let out an aggravated growl. "Can't you ask him about it some other time? We're going to be late!"

"It'll only take a second," she argued. "Go on without me. I'll be right there."

But she wasn't right there. In fact she didn't show up all period. And neither did Ryan.

When the bell rang ending the morning, I practically threw my test on Mrs. Adams' desk and bolted out of the room. I headed straight for the girls' washroom. If Liberty had skipped class, chances were that's where she was.

I pushed the door open and poked my head inside. There was a group of girls standing in front of the sinks, gabbing and doing their hair.

"Have you seen Liberty?" I asked them.

They shook their heads.

I let go of the door, but a voice from one of the cubicles made me push it open again.

"She's in the office."

"What's she doing there?" I said to myself as much as anyone.

"From the looks of her, crying," the voice said.

Crying! Why would she be crying? Then I had a thought.

Neither Ryan nor Liberty had been in history. Maybe they'd bumped into one another on the way to class and gotten into a fight.

"Thanks," I said and took off.

There was a crowd of kids milling outside the office by the front door. Even so, I saw Ryan right away. But before I could get to him, he bolted out of the school and climbed into his dad's van.

I frowned. He'd obviously been waiting for a ride. Even so, he'd taken off so fast it was like he was avoiding me. I pushed my way through the crowd to the office.

"Is Liberty here?" I said to my mom once I was inside.

She motioned for me to come around the counter. Then she got up from her desk and led the way to the counseling room.

"I called her father," she said in a lowered voice. "He's on his way to pick her up now." Then she placed a hand on the doorknob. "But she's pretty upset. I think she could use a friend. Just try not to get her any more worked up than she already is."

I was totally bewildered. "Why? What happened? Did she have an accident or something?"

Before Mom could answer, the door of the principal's office opened and Mr. Henderson—walking like a robot and looking white as a ghost—brushed past us. My mother took one look at him and pushed me into the counseling office.

"Never mind that now," she said. "Just try to keep Liberty calm."

That was easier said than done. Liberty was curled in a little ball on the couch, but the second she saw me she leaped to her feet, launched herself at me and started wailing. She was so upset it took me a good five minutes to get her quiet.

Then I asked, "What happened?" I didn't know what had set her off, but I was pretty sure it must have had something to do with either Ryan or Cody.

I couldn't have been more wrong.

New tears welled up in Liberty's eyes, and her shoulders started to shake.

"Mr....Mr....Hender...Henderson," she sobbed, "he...he...he...tried to rape me."

Chapter Six

I heard Liberty's father before I saw him. Of course, not having met him before, I couldn't be sure the voice bellowing outside the counseling room belonged to him, but the fact that it was threatening to kill Mr. Henderson seemed like a pretty good indication. And then when Liberty flew out the door and latched onto him, there wasn't much doubt.

Mr. Hayes was a tall, muscular man, and when he wrapped Liberty in his arms she practically disappeared. I stood quietly by as he whispered soothing words into her hair.

"It's okay, baby. It's okay, Liberty honey," he kept saying over and over. "Daddy's here. You're safe now." Then taking her head in both of his big hands, he kissed her forehead.

Liberty's face melted into something between relief and awe—the sort of expression you might expect to see on someone who'd just met God. That surprised me. I mean, I don't think I even have a look like the one Liberty was wearing, but if I did I certainly wouldn't use it on my dad.

I hadn't even finished thinking that thought when shame hit me like a bucket of icy water. I was shocked by my own cattiness. Liberty had practically been raped, and here I was criticizing her.

Clinging to one another, she and her dad headed for the principal's office and closed the door. I wouldn't say Mr. Hayes slammed it, but he definitely shut it with attitude. I couldn't help feeling a little sorry for Mr. Garvey.

At the same instant, Cody came skidding in from the hall.

"I heard what happened," he panted. "Where's Liberty? Is she all right?" Then his expression went from concern to anger. "I can't believe Mr. Henderson would do something like that! I just want to punch his head in."

Mom frowned and came around the counter.

"That kind of talk isn't going to solve anything," she scolded Cody. "Besides, at the moment we don't really know what happened. Until Mr. Garvey and the police make some inquiries, nobody is going to do anything—especially not you."

"Police!" I yelped. "Did Mr. Garvey call the police?"

"There's no choice in matters like this," Mom said as she shooed away the mob of kids outside the office. "Attempted rape is a very serious offense."

My mouth fell open. "Is Mr. Henderson going to go to jail?"

"There won't be anything to put in jail if I get my hands on him!" Cody growled through gritted teeth.

Mom gave Cody's arm an angry shake. "I told you, that's enough! You two shouldn't even be discussing this. Now go and eat your lunch. And don't go spreading stories you—"

That's when Liberty and her dad burst out of the principal's office.

"Mr. Hayes, please!" Mr. Garvey called after them. "You have to wait for the police."

"Like hell I do!" Liberty's father barked without slowing down. "I'm taking my daughter home!"

Afraid of getting mowed over, Mom and I both jumped out of the way.

"Liberty!" Cody called as she whisked past.

But Liberty might as well have been deaf. She didn't even look at him.

"Please pass the bread," Dad said. He slathered butter on a slice and asked, "So what happens now?"

We all turned to Mom. She gave us a *wait-a-second* look and made a big show of chewing and swallowing. Then she reached for her glass of water and took a sip. Finally she said, "Well, it looks like Liberty's father is going to press charges. That means the case will likely end up in court.

In the meantime, Dave Henderson is suspended."

"That's it?" Cody blurted. "The guy tries to rape Liberty and all that happens is he gets suspended? What kind of justice is that?"

"If he's guilty, he'll probably go to jail," Mom pointed out. "At the very least, he'll lose his job and maybe even his license to teach."

"That's *if* he's guilty," Dad said with emphasis.

"What do you mean 'if'?" Cody exploded. "There's no *if* about it! Liberty said he tried to rape her. Don't you think she would know?"

Dad put up his hand. "Calm down. I don't like men who force themselves on women any better than you do. All I'm saying is it's dangerous to jump to conclusions. Since I didn't witness what happened—and neither did you—I'm not willing to crucify Dave Henderson just yet. I'm sure there will be a complete police investigation."

"It's already underway," Mom said. "There were officers at the school all afternoon, interviewing people and checking out the band room. I imagine they were at the Hayes' house too." She looked at me and then Cody. "Has either of you spoken to Liberty this afternoon?"

"I tried," I said. "I phoned after school, but her mother said she was sleeping."

Mom nodded. "Of course. Poor thing. After all that's happened, she must be completely wrung out. We shouldn't bother her. It's just that your father got me thinking."

"About what?" Dad said.

"About witnesses. I was wondering if there'd been any."

After supper I called Ryan. I wanted to find out why he'd missed history. I also wanted to see if he knew anything more than I did about what had happened to Liberty. After all, he'd been standing outside the office when I got there. Maybe he'd seen Liberty arrive. Maybe he'd even talked to her.

"I just couldn't stay awake," he explained.

"No kidding," I replied. "I watched you go to math. You could barely walk."

"Yeah, well, then you won't be surprised to find out that I never made it to math. I passed an empty classroom on the way and couldn't resist going in. I figured if I could put my head down for forty minutes I'd be okay."

"Obviously the forty minutes stretched out a bit."

"You could say that. By the time I woke up, history class had already started."

"That's like two periods!" I exclaimed. "I can't believe nobody found you."

"Just lucky, I guess."

"Or unlucky—if you consider that you missed the test. What are you going to tell Mrs. Adams?"

Ryan sighed. "I was kind of hoping the truth would work."

I chuckled. "You never know. By the way, how's Hercules?"

"Lots better."

"That's good."

"Yeah. Doc Jensen gave him some medicine. Hopefully we'll both be able to sleep tonight."

"I saw you waiting for your dad outside the office. I waved, but I guess you didn't see me."

"Sorry."

"That's okay. I was just wondering if you'd been there when Liberty showed up. You heard about what happened between her and Mr. Henderson, right?"

Ryan didn't say anything.

"Ryan? Are you still there?"

He sighed. "Yup. I'm here."

"Were you there when Liberty went to the office?"

"Nope."

"You do know what Mr. Henderson tried to do though, don't you?"

Another pause. Another sigh. And then in a brittle voice Ryan said, "I know what Liberty *says* he tried to do."

Chapter Seven

I was kind of mad at Ryan. Though he hadn't come straight out with it, he'd pretty much called Liberty a liar. And that was so not like him. Ryan's the guy who usually sticks up for people. But when it came to Liberty, he couldn't seem to find enough rocks to throw at her. I think being on the outside of the group was getting to him.

I didn't like the situation either, but there wasn't much I could do about it. Ryan was determined to hate Liberty, and because everyone else liked her, he was the odd man out. As for Liberty, she was too busy with her own problems to notice what was going on with him.

After her traumatic experience, I totally expected Liberty to be away from school for a while. But she didn't miss a single day. Most of the time she rode the bus, but the day after the band room incident she arrived in her dad's red Porsche. As I watched her get out of the car, I wondered how everyone was going to act. Would the kids mob her with questions? Or would they keep their distance, whispering behind their hands? And what about me? Liberty had said I was her best friend, so I felt like I should be doing something to help her. I just didn't know what.

But I didn't have to wrestle with the problem for long. As usual, Liberty took matters into her own hands. As soon as she saw me she waved and headed over.

"How are you doing?" I asked when she reached me. I hoped my voice was cheerful enough to lift her spirits, but not so bubbly that it sounded like I was blowing off what had happened to her.

"I'm okay," she said.

I nodded and smiled tightly. Conversation had never been a problem for us before, but all of a sudden I found myself groping for something to say. The incident with Mr. Henderson had made Liberty seem like a stranger.

"I phoned you last night," I said.

Liberty flipped her hair back from her face. "I know. My mother told me."

"I guess you weren't up to taking calls."

She rolled her eyes. "I was fine. It was my parents who were wired.

59

Well, my dad anyway. To tell you the truth, I don't think my mother even knew what was going on. She basically lives on tranquilizers. Most of the time you could drop an anvil on her head and she wouldn't blink."

"I'm sorry," I said. "I didn't realize she was sick."

Liberty snorted. "Oh, she's sick all right, but not like you think. She spends so much time with her shrink that people think she works in his office. Anyway, let's not talk about her." And with a wave of Liberty's hand, Mrs. Hayes was gone. Then Liberty lowered her voice and said, "You'll never guess what happened when the police came to my house."

Instantly curious, I leaned in closer. "What?"

"Well, my dad was furious," she said. "Not with me, of course," she added quickly. "With Mr. Henderson. After we got home, he got madder and madder. He was just about to jump in his car and go looking for the guy when the police showed up."

"Why would your dad go after Mr. Henderson?"

Liberty shot me an incredulous look. "What do you think? To beat him up."

"You're kidding!" I gasped. Then I remembered that Cody had wanted to punch Mr. Henderson out too. A picture of our band teacher mashed to a pulp popped into my head. I winced.

"Anyway," Liberty continued, "it didn't happen because, like I said, the police came."

"I guess they asked you a bunch of questions, huh?"

"Tons!" she exclaimed. "After a while I was so confused I didn't know what I was saying anymore. That's when I started to cry. And that got my dad mad all over again. I thought he was going to beat the *police* up! He wouldn't let them ask me even one more thing. He said they were bullying me, and if they didn't leave right that second, he was going to throw them out and charge them with harassment."

"What happened then?"

Liberty shrugged. "Nothing. They left. Then my dad ran me a bubble bath and made me spend the rest of the day in bed. He brought me tea and scones and sat with me the whole time. I felt like a princess. He even canceled an important business trip so I wouldn't have to go through this alone."

I wanted to say, *What about your mom? Wouldn't she be with you?* But it didn't seem like Mrs. Hayes was Liberty's favorite person, so I kept my mouth shut.

Out of the corner of my eye I saw Cody coming our way. I knew he was anxious to talk to Liberty, but I also knew he was worried about saying the wrong thing and upsetting her all over again. Considering her mood, I didn't see a problem.

I nodded in Cody's direction. "Here comes your boyfriend."

It was like I'd flipped a switch. Liberty dropped her books and spun around. "Oh, Cody!" she cried, running at him and throwing her arms around his neck. "Oh, Cody, it was so awful."

After school Cody rode the bus with Liberty, so Mom dragged me to the grocery store with her.

"I just need to pick up a few things," she said. Half an hour later she was still going strong. In an effort to speed up the process, I sneaked a peek at her list and headed for the pasta aisle. In three minutes I was back, dumping the spaghetti into the cart.

"Not on the tomatoes, Val!" Mom complained.

"Oops. Sorry," I said, quickly rearranging the groceries. "What else do you need?"

She didn't even look up from the green beans she was picking through. "Just a couple of onions."

"Where are they?" I said, tearing a plastic bag from a roll and grabbing a twist tie.

"Right next to the potatoes."

"Got it." I turned to go, but froze in mid-stride.

Mom looked up. "What's the matter?"

"Over there by the carrots," I whispered out of the side of my mouth. "That's Mr. Henderson's wife."

Mom glanced over. "So?"

"So I can't believe she's here! Look. People are staring at her and she's acting like she doesn't even notice."

Mom shook her head and went back to her beans. "What do you expect her to do?" she muttered.

I rolled my eyes. My mother was so clued out.

"Her husband tried to rape a student! She has to know everyone in town is talking about it."

"Well, shame on them if they are," Mom snapped. "And shame on you too. Obviously you didn't hear a word your father said last night. You've already found your teacher guilty—and by the looks of it, his family too. The Hendersons are under enough stress without having to worry about malicious gossip."

Then she pushed past me and got the onions herself.

Chapter Eight

The Tattler is the town paper. It comes out once a week, but because not a lot happens in Sutter's Crossing, there isn't usually much to it. So the story about Liberty and Mr. Henderson should have been splashed all over the front page. But it wasn't. In fact, the only mention of it was a measly couple of sentences near the back.

"Look." I flipped the paper across the table to Cody. It landed on top of his math homework.

"Do you mind?" He glared at me from under lowered eyebrows.

"Well, excuse me," I sniped back. "I thought you might be interested in the article about Liberty."

Cody put down his pencil and picked up the paper.

"Where?" he said, scanning the page.

I reached across the mound of school books and tapped the article with my pen. "This one here—*Local Teacher Suspended.*"

Cody read the article out loud.

"Just a month into the school year, Clarence Cobb Regional Secondary School is already short a teacher. David Henderson, the band instructor, was suspended last week following allegations of behavioral misconduct involving a student. School principal, Brian Garvey, declined to comment, and district super-intendent, Walter Bishop, would say only that the matter was under investi-gation. The name of the student is being withheld."

Cody threw the paper down in disgust. "Behavioral misconduct—what a bunch of crap! Why don't they just say what really happened? The creep tried to rape Liberty! It's like everybody is trying to protect him. Why? Liberty is the victim here—not Henderson. Doesn't anybody care what happened to her?"

I thought about that for a few seconds. What *had* happened to her? I still didn't really know. Every kid in the school seemed to have their own version of what had gone on in the band room that morning—but I hadn't actually heard the story from Liberty. All she'd talked about were her feelings and what had occurred afterward with the police and her father. Since I was supposed to be her best friend, I thought she would have confided in me, but she hadn't—at least not so far. Maybe the memory of being attacked was too painful. Or maybe—I looked across the table at Cody—maybe she'd told someone else.

Subtlety is wasted on my brother, so I didn't even go through the motions. "Has Liberty told you what Mr. Henderson did to her?" I said point-blank.

Another glare from under the eyebrows. "Of course," he sneered. "I'm her boyfriend—remember?"

"I'm talking about details," I said bluntly. "Has she given you a blow-by-blow account of things?"

Cody screwed up his face as if he were in pain. "What are you—a reporter?"

I shook my head. "Supposedly I'm Liberty's friend. But the only thing she's told me is that she stayed after class to ask Mr. Henderson something about her clarinet. The next thing she knew, he was coming on to her and wouldn't take 'no' for an answer."

"What more do you need to know?"

"I told you—details. Like what did he say to Liberty? What did she say to him? Did he try to grab her? Did she scream? How far did he get? How long did it take? You know—details!"

Cody threw down his pencil. "You're a pervert!"

"I am not. I just think it's strange that nobody knows any of this stuff."

"If it happened to you, would you want the world to know?" he shot back.

"I might if I was Liberty," I muttered under my breath.

But Cody had heard me. "What's that supposed to mean?" he demanded.

"Nothing," I said quickly. I kicked myself for thinking such a mean thought and—even worse—for letting it leak out of my mouth.

"Then why did you say it?"

"Because I'm stupid."

"No kidding."

I ignored the dig.

"It's just that Liberty isn't exactly a low-profile person, is she?" I chose my words more carefully this time. "She likes being in the middle of things. I'm not saying that's a bad thing," I added hastily, noting the way Cody's eyes had narrowed and his nostrils were puffing in and out like a racehorse's. "It just seems like she would have told somebody what had gone on."

"She did," he said flatly. "The police."

I strapped on my helmet and wheeled my bike out of the shed. Then I inhaled deeply. There was a definite nip of autumn in the air, but the sun was shining, the sky was blue, and it felt like the whole world was smiling. It was just too good a morning to stay indoors. Besides, if I hung around the house, Mom was bound to find work for me, and that was not how I wanted to spend my Saturday.

I hadn't intended to ride over to Ryan's place. I mean, he lives a good seven miles away. It just sort of happened. I guess I was feeling energetic—and maybe a bit guilty about how little I'd seen of him lately. Even though we were in most of the same classes, we didn't sit near enough to talk, and once the bell rang, Ryan always seemed to disappear.

As I pedaled up the long dirt driveway to his house, I spotted him in the corral, brushing Hercules. He saw me and waved.

"What brings you out to the boonies?" he asked as I climbed the fence and plunked down on the top rail.

"Do I need a reason?" I grinned. "Can't a friend visit a friend?"

Ryan didn't answer, but the way he looked at me over Hercules's back made me wish I could take back that last sentence.

"We haven't seen much of each other lately," I tried again more honestly.

"You know where to find me," he said, but he sounded so far away it hurt. I hated this! When had Ryan and I started tiptoeing around each other? We used to be able to talk about anything! And now…well…and now we couldn't. If we didn't fix things soon, it would be too late.

"Ryan," I blurted, "why aren't we friends anymore?"

"We are friends," he said.

If that was true, why was he being so cold? He wouldn't even look at me. Maybe it was already too late. Misery settled over me like a lead overcoat.

"Not friends like we used to be," I said.

"Things change."

"The only change is Liberty Hayes. For some reason that I don't understand—and you won't explain—you don't like her."

I waited for him to answer, but he just kept brushing Hercules.

"Well, I *do* like her!" I shouted in an effort to bring Ryan back to life.

"It's a free country," he shrugged.

I tried again, determined to get through to him. "Why are you being so difficult about this? You have no good reason to dislike Liberty. If anything, I would think you'd feel sorry for her after what Mr. Henderson did."

That hit a nerve. Ryan threw the brush to the ground. Then, looking as if he was about to murder someone, he came striding toward me. I didn't know whether to scream or run, but he was in my face so fast, I didn't have time to do either.

"Mr. Henderson didn't do anything!" he yelled. "It's all just a big, fat lie!"

"You don't know that!" I wailed. What was the matter with Ryan? Why couldn't he just give up on this hate he had for Liberty?

"Oh, yes I do."

"How could you?"

"Easy," he growled, staring at me so hard I started to squirm. "I was there."

Chapter Nine

"What?"

"You heard me. I was there."

"You couldn't have been." I shook my head. I didn't want to call Ryan a liar, but what he was saying didn't make sense. "You told me you fell asleep in an empty classroom during first period and didn't wake up until after history had started."

"That's right. It just so happens that the classroom I fell asleep in was band."

I hadn't even considered that possibility, so suddenly I didn't have anything to say. But after I'd thought about it for a few seconds, I frowned. "Uh-uh. That can't be. The band room might have been empty first period, but we had class in there second period, and you were definitely not there. I know, because I looked for you."

"Well, you obviously didn't look in practice booth three, because that's where I was. I figured it would be the perfect place for a nap. It's soundproof, there's carpet on the floor, and when the light's off, it's totally dark. I slept like a rock. I never even knew there was a class going on."

Ryan had barely been able to keep his eyes open during homeroom, so it was easy to see how he could've slept through band. But two hours isn't long to crash when you've been up all night.

If forty kids on tubas, trumpets and drums couldn't wake him, it seemed unlikely that he'd suddenly come to when there was only Liberty and Mr. Henderson in the room.

"Okay. So what woke you up?" Even I heard the suspicion in my voice.

Ryan's eyebrows shot up. "You don't believe me, do you—*friend*?"

I don't know if it was the way he said "friend" or the accusing look in his eyes, but suddenly I felt like he'd stuck a knife in my ribs. For a few seconds I just stood there gaping at him.

"That's so mean, Ryan." My voice trembled when I finally found it again. "It's mean and totally unfair."

He kicked the fence post so hard the rail I was sitting on vibrated.

"You should talk!" His eyes flashed angrily. "You come here claiming to be my friend, and in the next breath you accuse me of lying! If you ask me, you're the one who's being mean and unfair." He turned away in disgust and started marching back toward Hercules.

Now *I* was angry. "Oh no you don't," I muttered, jumping down from the fence and chasing after him. I grabbed his arm and spun him around. Then I jammed my fists onto my hips and glared at him.

"What do you expect?" I growled. "You've made it clear to everybody in town that you hate Liberty. And now— an entire week after the attack—you suddenly remember that you witnessed the whole thing! And, *of course*, Liberty's the one to blame. Give me a break, Ryan. If I were telling you that, would *you* believe it?"

The morning got very quiet. We stood facing each other like a couple of edgy gunslingers.

Ryan fired first. "Yes," he said. "I would believe it, because you're my friend—and friends don't lie."

Zing! A clean shot right through the heart.

I didn't fall down, but it sure felt like I was dying. Or maybe it was our friendship that was dying. And if it was, it was my fault. Somewhere along the way I'd forgotten how to be a friend.

Hot tears burned my eyes. I didn't want Ryan to see me cry, so I turned and started running for the fence.

But I never got there.

I didn't even realize Ryan had moved until he was standing between me and the gate. I went to swerve around him, but he grabbed both my arms and cut off my escape. I tried to break free. That didn't work either. Finally I stopped struggling and stared down at my feet, waiting for Ryan to dump on me some more.

"Look at me," he said.

I couldn't.

He gave my shoulders a shake. "Look at me!"

Jolted from self-pity to alarm, I did as I was told. A tear slid from my eye. With my arms pinned to my sides, there was nothing I could do about it.

Ryan watched it roll down my cheek and then he frowned. "Friends don't lie," he said quietly. Then he added, "And they don't make each other cry." He let go of my arms. "I'm sorry, Val."

I couldn't believe my ears. Had Ryan just apologized?

"What did you say?"

"I said I'm sorry," he repeated.

"You are?" I echoed in disbelief.

He nodded.

"Does that mean we're still friends?" I sniffed.

Ryan stuffed his hands into his pockets. "Unless you don't want to be."

Suddenly I couldn't speak for the stranglehold my heart had on my throat. I just threw my arms around Ryan and wiped my tears on his shirt.

Once we'd made up, Ryan told me what had happened in the band room. He explained how he'd set his watch alarm to go off just before the end of second period. When he woke up he'd opened the door a crack so he could peek out.

The kids left in dribs and drabs, and soon Liberty and Mr. Henderson were the only ones there. With only three minutes between classes, Ryan was antsy to get going. But if he showed himself he'd have to explain why he'd missed band, and he didn't want to do that. So he just stayed put and waited.

At first everything seemed pretty normal. Liberty explained the problem with her clarinet, and Mr. Henderson checked it out. But he couldn't find anything wrong, so he gave it back and started packing up his briefcase.

Liberty put her clarinet away, but instead of heading to history, she kept hanging around. At first she leaned against the desk. Then she sat on the corner of it, and when Mr. Henderson walked by, she jumped up in such a hurry that she fell into him with her breasts—accidentally on purpose, according to Ryan.

Of course, they both apologized all over the place, and Mr. Henderson told Liberty to get to her next class. She pouted but started to gather up her things. Until Mr. Henderson went into the instrument room. That's when Liberty undid a couple of buttons on her shirt and followed him.

They weren't in there long. In less than two minutes, Mr. Henderson came flying out as if wild horses were chasing him. And Liberty was right behind him.

Red in the face, Mr. Henderson stood so his desk was between the two of them and said hoarsely, "I think you'd better leave."

For a few seconds Liberty just stared daggers at him. Then, without even picking up her things, she ran to the door. But as she grabbed the knob, she looked back and growled, "You'll be sorry."

Chapter Ten

Though I believed Ryan's story, I still wasn't willing to turn against Liberty. For one thing, Ryan hadn't seen her do anything except unbutton her blouse. It was a dumb thing to do, but it didn't prove she was the one who had done the attacking. Whatever had happened between her and Mr. Henderson, it had happened in the instrument room, and Ryan said himself that he couldn't see in there. Mr. Henderson might have tried to molest Liberty. Or Liberty might have come on to him. There was no way of knowing.

The other thing in Liberty's favor was the fact that Ryan wasn't willing to go to the authorities with what he knew.

"It's my word against hers," he said when I called him on it. "Everybody knows I don't like Liberty. They'll just think I'm trying to get her in trouble. Besides, like you said, I didn't actually see what happened. I'm sure Mr. Henderson is innocent, but I can't prove it."

"I know this is changing the subject," I said, "but why *don't* you like Liberty? It's like you've hated her from the second I introduced you."

Ryan shook his head. "No. I hated her way before that."

My mouth dropped open. "Huh?"

"I met Liberty before you introduced us."

"Huh?" I said again. "When? Where? How?"

"On the connector flight from Vancouver to Kamloops on my way back from California. It was when Liberty and her mom were coming to Sutter's Crossing. Liberty had the seat next to mine. During the flight she came on to me like I was a movie star or something. And I fell for it." He grimaced. "Boy, did I fall for it! I can't believe I was so gullible. I even gave her my phone number. But when the plane touched down in Kelowna, the lady across the aisle from Liberty got off, and a guy got on in her place. And suddenly it was like I'd disappeared. Liberty only had eyes for him."

I was stunned. For a few seconds all I could do was blink. "Why didn't you tell me this before?" I said finally.

Ryan frowned. "It's not exactly the sort of thing a guy wants to get around."

Up until then I'd been completely on Liberty's side. But now I didn't know what to believe. Knowing Liberty, I was almost certain she'd been trying to get Mr. Henderson to notice her. She'd told me herself she thought he was hot. And though I couldn't believe she'd actually want to make out with him, I wouldn't put it past her to be a tease. I mean, anybody who wears a see-through blouse isn't going to think twice about undoing a couple of buttons.

The thing is, no matter how much I thought about it, I couldn't picture Mr. Henderson taking advantage of the situation. Some male teachers give you the creeps with the way they look at you, but Mr. Henderson wasn't like that. He was friendly with all the kids—

girls *and* guys—but in a strictly teacher-student kind of way.

So maybe he *hadn't* attacked Liberty. In fact, I'd almost talked myself into the idea, when—partway through dinner a few nights later—my mother announced that Mrs. Henderson had left town. Mom didn't know where she'd gone, or why, but considering the circumstances it seemed pretty obvious to me. The lady had walked out. And suddenly I found myself switching sides again. If Mr. Henderson's own wife didn't believe he was innocent, why should I?

Of course, two days later I changed my mind again. In fact, by the time the middle of October rolled around, I must have flip-flopped fifty times. The situation was dragging on forever, and I was beginning to wonder if it was ever going to get settled. Liberty's dad hadn't dropped the charges, but there was no court date in sight. And Mr. Henderson was still suspended.

Whenever I went down Mason Street, I'd peer at his house. Not that there was much to see. Since Mrs. Henderson had moved out there were no toys on the grass and no laundry drying on the line. The drapes were closed; the yard was deserted. If it weren't for Mr. Henderson's car in the driveway, you would've thought he'd left town too. But I knew he hadn't. Otherwise his fence wouldn't have had RAPIST spray-painted across it, and his car wouldn't have gotten egged.

The third Saturday in October is when Sutter's Crossing holds its annual Autumn Supper and Dance at the community hall. It's a big deal, and everybody attends. I mean *everybody*. Everybody except Mr. Henderson, that is.

Considering I hadn't seen him once since he'd been suspended, I shouldn't have been surprised. It's just that it felt wrong. Everyone else in town was in the community center, having a good time, and he was hidden away in his little house, all alone.

The sound of rhythmic clapping drew my attention to the dance floor. While Marty Mezner and the Hoedown Cowboys rocked the hall with the "Beer Barrel Polka," a bunch of people stood in a big circle keeping the beat. I caught a glimpse of dancers beyond them and squeezed through to the front of the crowd for a better look.

It was Liberty and her dad! And they had the floor all to themselves. Round and round they whirled, so close to the crowd that I could feel the breeze that followed them. They were both grinning, and every once in a while—when Mr. Hayes would put them into a particularly fast spin—Liberty would throw back her head, sending peals of laughter rippling into the air with the music.

Cody was standing on the other side of the circle, almost directly across from me. Beside him was Mrs. Hayes. She was clapping along with everyone else, but the furrow between her eyebrows said she wasn't enjoying the show. In fact, she slipped out of the circle and walked back to her table before the music ended.

When the song was over, the crowd applauded, and Liberty and her dad bowed. Then the band announced it was taking a break, someone turned on a CD player, and Faith Hill started singing a slow, romantic song. Liberty put her arms out to her dad again, but Cody appeared and claimed the dance instead. Mr. Hayes smiled and patted him on the back and then returned to his seat.

I spotted Ryan holding up the wall by the punch bowl, so I headed over to keep him company. We gabbed for a bit, but soon he headed for the exit to walk off his three helpings of supper.

So I turned back to the dance floor. It was another slow song, and this time Liberty's parents were dancing together. As they floated by, Mr. Hayes whispered something in Mrs. Hayes's ear, and suddenly it was like there was a spotlight shining on her. Her whole face lit up, and when she smiled, she looked really, really pretty.

I peered around for my brother and Liberty. I didn't see Cody, but Liberty was waltzing with Jason Kaufmann. I was surprised. For one thing, I thought slow dances were reserved for Cody. For another thing, Jason is in college— he only comes home on weekends—so I didn't see how he and Liberty even knew each other. And for a third thing, the two of them were dancing awfully close. Somehow I didn't think Cody would appreciate that.

"Can I call you next time I'm home for the weekend?" I heard Jason ask when he walked Liberty off the floor at the end of the song.

"If you like." Liberty smiled.

I frowned. I was pretty sure Cody wouldn't appreciate that either.

Chapter Eleven

A few minutes later Cody walked in from the parking lot with some of his friends. Judging from the smile on his face, he had no clue what had been going on while he'd been gone.

I considered telling him, but that would make me look like I was trying to stir up trouble—*which I wasn't!* After all, what I'd overheard might have been perfectly innocent. And even if it wasn't, it was only my word against Liberty's. So why would Cody want to believe me?

Suddenly reality smacked me right between the eyes, and I knew exactly why Ryan had kept quiet about what he'd seen in the band room. It didn't matter whether you were telling the truth or not if no one believed you. I shuddered. Was that how Mr. Henderson felt too?

The next thing I knew there was another slow song, and Cody and Liberty were wrapped around each other on the dance floor. I breathed a sigh of relief. I'd obviously been suspicious for nothing. Thank goodness I'd kept my mouth shut.

Wrong!

The very next afternoon I saw Liberty riding in Jason Kaufmann's car, and when I got home, Cody told me Liberty had broken up with him.

I couldn't believe it!

Neither could Cody. Apparently Liberty hadn't even given him a reason. All she'd said was she didn't want to go out with him anymore. Cody was crushed. Oh, he tried to hide it, but I know my brother. And even though there are times when I want to mash his face into a cow pie, I couldn't help feeling sorry for him.

Not because he was going to die of a broken heart. I mean, couples break up all the time, and he and Liberty hadn't been going out that long. But the way Liberty had dumped him was heartless. Cody's pride had taken a real kicking. And considering how he'd stuck up for her through the whole molestation thing, it really ticked me off.

I couldn't help thinking about the way Liberty had dissed Ryan on the plane. Was that how it was with Cody too? Had Liberty dumped him because a college guy suddenly caught her interest?

I didn't know the answer, but I intended to find out.

Unfortunately, that was easier said than done.

The next morning I waited in my usual spot outside the main doors of the school. But when Liberty got off the bus, she didn't head over. Instead, she walked off with some grade eleven girls. I admit I was surprised, but it didn't bother me. After all, I couldn't really ask her about Cody with a bunch of other people listening in.

So I waited for her at her locker. Good plan, except Liberty never showed. We had only one class together that morning, so I made up my mind to talk with her then. That didn't work out either. Even though we always sat together, the chairs on either side of her were taken by the time I got there.

When she walked right past me at lunchtime and sat at another table, the light finally went on. Liberty was avoiding me. It looked like Cody wasn't the only one who'd been dumped.

All afternoon I thought about that—which is probably why I couldn't get any formulas to balance in chemistry and why I let in four goals during a soccer game in phys ed. And though being snubbed by Liberty shocked and embarrassed me, those feelings soon changed to anger. The more I thought about things, the angrier I got.

Liberty had used me. She'd used me to get to Cody, and she'd used me to get in with the other kids at school. And now that she didn't need me anymore, she was tossing me away like an empty candy bar wrapper. By the time the last bell rang I was so mad it was a wonder steam wasn't pouring out of my ears. If I'd passed Liberty in the hall at that moment I would probably have punched her in the nose.

I made a quick trip to my locker and then poked my head into the office to let Mom know I'd be taking the bus home.

As I climbed aboard, I could see Liberty at the back with her new grade eleven friends. I took a seat near the front beside Sarah Shaw. When the bus stopped at the end of Liberty's driveway, I didn't even watch her leave. A quarter mile down the road, I got off with Sarah. Since my stop was another two miles away, Sarah was more than a little surprised. But I crossed my fingers behind my back and explained that I'd left something at Liberty's that I needed right away. I didn't tell her it was my self-respect.

With my eyes fixed blindly on the rolling purple hills ahead, and my mind focused on what I was going to say, I began the trek back to Liberty's house. I played out the different ways the conversation might go. At first, all I could see was me biting Liberty's head off.

That was the least she deserved! But the closer I got to her house, the less angry I got, and the more reasonable the conversations taking place in my head became.

I'd explain how hurt Cody and I were, and Liberty would apologize. She might even cry. She'd admit she'd made a mistake dumping Cody, and she'd beg me to help her get him back. Then she'd confess how embarrassed she was, and that was why she'd avoided me all day.

I sighed and raked my hand through a tall clump of golden horsetails at the side of the road. *Yeah, right!*

At the bottom of Liberty's driveway I stopped. I wasn't chickening out or anything. I just needed a minute to get my engines totally revved—kind of like an airplane that sits at the end of the runway for a second before barreling ahead for takeoff.

Chapter Twelve

Mrs. Hayes was frowning as she answered the door. For a second it looked like she wasn't going to let me in. But then her frown dissolved and she pointed to the staircase behind her.

"Liberty's in her room," she said. "Go on up."

Liberty didn't hear me coming. It was a good minute before she noticed me standing in the doorway. She was sprawled across her bed, talking on the phone. Her eyes were sparkling and there was laughter in her voice. She looked so much like the Liberty I was used to that I almost forgot why I'd come. But then she saw me, and her expression became hard as stone.

"I'll have to call you back," she told the person on the other end of the phone. She pushed herself up to a sitting position and glared at me. "How did you get in here?" Then she bellowed into the hallway behind me. "Mother!" And again. "Mother!"

"Save your breath," I said. "I'm not staying."

"What do you want?" Liberty snarled. "And make it fast. I have things to do." As if to prove her point, she got to her feet and stalked across the room to her dresser.

"That's a nice way to talk to your *best friend*."

Liberty didn't even have the decency to look embarrassed. She just shot me a pitying glance and began rummaging through a drawer.

"You wish," she muttered.

"Actually, I don't," I said.

That caught her attention, and the smug look on her face slipped. But only for a second.

"What do you want?" she demanded again.

"I want to know why you broke up with Cody."

Liberty stopped rummaging and regarded me with amusement. Then she stuck her bottom lip out in an exaggerated pout. "Why? Did Cody get his little feelings hurt? Is he crying? Did he send you over here to beg me to take him back?"

It was all I could do not to pounce on Liberty and scratch her eyes out. I still don't know how I managed to keep my cool. But I did. "Answer my question," I said.

Liberty let out an enormous sigh. "I would have thought it was obvious. Cody is a little boy. And I'm looking for a man."

I felt my eyebrows jump, but the rest of me stayed perfectly still.

"Like Jason Kaufmann?" I said snidely. "Is that your idea of a man— *this week*?"

A smile played at the corners of Liberty's mouth. "Maybe." She shrugged. "As soon as I find out, I'll let you know." Then she turned back to her dresser.

"Or are you looking for someone more like Mr. Henderson?"

I don't even remember thinking those words, never mind saying them out loud! But I must have, because Liberty grabbed the edge of the drawer so tightly her knuckles went white.

"You don't know what you're talking about," she snapped, but she didn't sound quite as confident as she had before.

"Well, you see, that's the thing," I said in a buttery voice. "I *do* know." I watched Liberty's back stiffen. "Because Ryan told me. And *he* knows because he saw you. He was in the band room that morning—in one of the practice booths. He saw you unbutton your blouse, and he saw you throw yourself at Mr. Henderson. He also saw Mr. Henderson reject you." That last part wasn't completely true, but Liberty didn't know that.

She spun around. Judging from the horrified expression on her face, I'd guessed right.

I didn't even try to hide my pleasure. In fact, I couldn't resist rubbing a little salt into the wound. "I guess Mr. Henderson isn't interested in little girls."

I expected a smart comeback like, *It's his loss!* But for once, Liberty was speechless. I knew I had the answers I'd come for.

So I turned around—and walked right into Mrs. Hayes. I mumbled an apology, but she didn't hear me. She didn't see me either. It was like I wasn't even there. Her eyes were totally glued on Liberty. And they were flashing fire. It's a wonder the whole room didn't burst into flame.

For once, I was glad I wasn't Liberty.

Cody picked me up about a mile from home.

"So, did you rearrange her face?" he asked as I slid onto the seat beside him.

"Whose face?"

"Liberty's. You were just at her house, weren't you?"

"How do you know?" I said, unable to keep the amazement out of my voice.

He grinned. "Easy. I'm smart."

"Since when?"

His grin got bigger. "Since I dumped Liberty."

I just about choked. "Excuse me. I hate to burst your bubble, but she's the one who broke up with you—remember?"

Cody shrugged. "She must've found out I was going to dump her and beat me to it so she wouldn't look bad."

I rolled my eyes. "Right, Romeo. And why would *you* dump *her*?"

He shrugged again. "I didn't like the competition."

"You mean Jason Kaufmann?"

"I mean her dad."

"Say what?"

"Mr. Hayes. When Liberty and I were together, that's all she talked about. It was like she was using me to make him jealous or something. And when it didn't work, she dumped me. It's kind of sick, don't you think?"

"Yeah," I mumbled. "Sick and sad."

That night I called Ryan. After I told him what had happened at Liberty's house, we decided Mr. Henderson had been a victim long enough. It was time to set the record straight.

When my mom heard the story, she immediately phoned Mr. Garvey. Suddenly Ryan and I had an early morning appointment at the office. All night I tossed and turned, thinking about it. I knew Ryan and I were doing the right thing, but that didn't stop me from worrying. After all, we were crossing Liberty, and look what had happened to Mr. Henderson when he'd tried it.

By the next morning I was a wreck. I thought my stomach was as knotted up as it could get, but when the office door swung open and Liberty's mom walked in, it snarled up a little bit more.

Mrs. Hayes looked every bit as fierce as she had the last time I'd seen her. She walked up to the counter and started talking to my mother. She said an unexpected business development required the family to leave Sutter's Crossing immediately. She'd arrange for Liberty's things to be picked up later. Then she placed two envelopes on the counter and left.

From where I was sitting, I could see the top envelope. It was addressed to Mr. Henderson. And it was in Liberty's handwriting. The second envelope was a mystery. At least it was until morning announcements.

That's when Mr. Garvey read it over the public address system for the whole school to hear. It was from Liberty too. In it she admitted she'd lied about Mr. Henderson trying to molest her, and she apologized to everyone for what she'd done.

I figured Liberty had been forced to write those letters, but since her dad was out of town, it had to have been her mother who'd done the forcing. It was probably the first time Mrs. Hayes had made Liberty do anything in her whole life. But I had a feeling it wouldn't be the last.

"So when will Mr. Henderson be back at school?" I asked my mom as we drove home that day.

She shook her head. "He won't."

"What do you mean?" I demanded. "Liberty confessed. They can't take Mr. Henderson's job away now!"

"No, they can't. But it doesn't matter. He handed in his resignation. He's going after his wife to try and salvage what's left of his marriage."

"But he's innocent!" I insisted. "Why doesn't Mrs. Henderson just come back?"

Mom sighed. "It's not that easy. When something like trust gets broken, it's a hard thing to fix."

Though I didn't like it, I knew she was right. My friendship with Ryan was proof of that. I shuddered to think how close I'd come to losing it.

Part of me wanted to blame Liberty for everything that had happened, but I couldn't.

I'm not saying she was innocent. She wasn't. She'd blown in and out of Sutter's Crossing like a tornado—causing about the same amount of damage. The thing is, she hadn't done it alone. Cody, Ryan, me, Liberty's parents, Mrs. Henderson, the kids at school, people in the community—we were all partly to blame for the things that had happened. If Liberty had manipulated us, it's because we let her.

Though I hated to admit it, I knew we were partly responsible for the business with Mr. Henderson too. We should have stood up for him, but we hadn't. Now all we could do was hope he could put his life back together.

Which just left Liberty. Amazingly, my feelings about her were still confused. I didn't admire her anymore, and I sure didn't envy her. But I didn't hate her either. What was the point? She was gone, and the trouble she'd caused was gone with her. And that's because the trouble with Liberty *was Liberty.*

A former teacher turned writer and reviewer, Kristin Butcher is the author of numerous popular books for teens, including *The Hemingway Tradition,* and *Zee's Way* in the Orca Soundings series. Kristin lives in Campbell River, British Columbia.

orca soundings

9781554698455 $9.95 PB
9781554698462 $16.95 LIB

March has a perfect life: beauty, popularity, a great job, a loving family and a hot boyfriend. So when she discovers that her boyfriend is cheating on her, she is hurt and enraged. When she lashes out at him, he falls and is badly injured. March panics, flees the scene and then watches her perfect life spiral out of control. In a misguided attempt to atone for her crime, March changes her appearance, quits her job and tries to become invisible, until an unlikely friendship and a new job force her to re-engage with life.

orca soundings

9781554692729 9.95 PB
9781554699766 16.95 LIB

Tara's sister died a year ago, on the day that Tara didn't answer her phone when Hannah called. And Hannah stepped in front of a bus. Now Tara lives with the guilt of wondering if things would be different if she had been there when Hannah needed her most. Competing in slam poetry competitions is the only way Tara can keep her sister's memory alive and deal with all the unanswered questions. But at some point, Tara is going to have to let Hannah rest in peace and she will need to find a way to move on.

orca soundings

9781554698936 $9.95 PB
9781554698943 $16.95 LIB

Jenessa's a thrill seeker by nature. Anything fast, she's all over it. Angry and blaming herself for her best friend's death, Jenessa escapes to the sanctuary of her car and the freedom of the open road, where she can outrun her memories…if only for a while. She finds a kindred spirit in Dmitri, a warm-hearted speed demon who races at the track. But when Jenessa falls in with a group of street racers—and its irresistible leader, Cody—she finds herself caught up in a web of escalating danger.

Titles in the Series

orca soundings